THE
LITTLE PRINCES

JOHN MELADY

Cover by Laszlo Gal

Scholastic-TAB Publications Ltd.

Scholastic-TAB Publications Ltd.
123 Newkirk Road, Richmond Hill, Ontario, Canada L4C 3G5

Scholastic Inc.
730 Broadway, New York, NY 10003, USA

Ashton Scholastic Limited
165 Marua Road, Panmure, PO Box 12328, Auckland 6, New
Zealand

Ashton Scholastic Pty Limited
PO Box 579, Gosford, NSW 2250, Australia

Scholastic Publications Ltd.
Holly Walk, Leamington Spa, Warwickshire CV32 4LS,
England

Canadian Cataloguing in Publication Data
Melady, John.
    The little princes

ISBN 0-590-71802-9

1. Edward V, King of England, 1470-1483 - Juvenile
fiction. 2. Richard, Duke of York, 1473-1483 -
Juvenile fiction. 3. Richard III, King of England,
1452-1485 - Juvenile fiction. 4. Great Britain -
History - Richard III, 1483-1485 - Juvenile fiction.
5. Great Britain - Kings and rulers - Biography -
Juvenile fiction. I. Title.

PS8576.E435L58 1988   jC813'.54   C87-095206-4
PZ7.M435Li 1988

8 7 6 5 4 3 2 1   Printed in Canada   8 9/8 0 1 2 3 4/9
Manufactured by Webcom Limited

In memory of my parents
Maurice and Mary Melady

By the same author:

Explosion
Escape From Canada!
Korea: Canada's Forgotten War
Cross of Valour
Overtime, Overdue: The Bill Barilko Story

Prologue

In 1483, Edward IV, king of England, suddenly died of a mysterious ailment. In his will he named his brother Richard, Duke of Gloucester, Royal Protector to his twelve-year-old son and heir, Edward. Immediately after the king's death, Gloucester arranged for the young Edward to be lodged in the Royal Apartments in the Tower of London until his coronation. A little later, his nine-year-old brother joined him.

Not long after that, they vanished from the face of the earth.

Just what happened to the two little princes is one of English history's greatest unsolved mysteries.

Were they simply innocent victims of the prevailing Wars of the Roses? Or did their disappearance have less to do with the bitter struggle between the white rose of York and the red rose of Lancaster than it did with one man's zeal and lust for power within the Royal House of York itself?

What follows is one author's account of the fate of the little princes in the Tower.

Chapter 1

It was late evening when the messengers arrived. The castle doors were closed and the servants had already removed the supper dishes. Far to the west, the April sun had disappeared and the Welsh countryside was blanketed in darkness.

The gateman heard them first.

"Open up! Open up in the name of the king!"

The gateman peered into the gloom. Two horsemen were galloping full speed towards the castle, shouting as they came.

"Open the doors. We have news for Lord Rivers. Open the doors!"

The gateman hesitated. He could not tell in the darkness just who the two men were. Their urgency seemed real enough, but then it could also be a ruse. He looked into the blackness beyond them to try and see if they were alone.

"Open up! Open up in the name of the king! You will pay dearly if Lord Rivers does not receive our news!"

The gateman hastily made up his mind.

He swung the doors wide. The riders charged through, the hooves of their horses pounding thecourtyard as they raced to the inner door.

A servant hurried to the threshold.

"Fetch Lord Rivers," shouted one of the riders. "At once!"

Instantly, the servant disappeared.

A few minutes later Rivers, Lord of Ludlow Castle and brother to the queen of England, appeared at the door. He was a tall man, slightly stooped. A shock of dark hair was swept back from his forehead. His expression was sharp and alert. When he saw the strangers, his eyes quickly narrowed with suspicion.

"Yes? What is it?" he barked. "Who are you? What are you doing here?"

The first rider cleared his throat.

"My Lord, my Lord," he panted, "not four days ago, in this year of Our Lord 1483, His Majesty King Edward IV of England died at Westminster Palace after a sudden illness."

Lord Rivers inhaled sharply.

"Died?" he gasped. "You are sure?"

"Yes m'Lord," repeated the messenger. "We came here by order of Her Majesty the Queen herself. We are instructed to tell you that but one week since, the king took to his bed complaining of a pain in his side. The doctors did all they could for him, but a mere two days later he was dead. They are not sure even now what it was that ailed him. They say only that they have seen the illness before — and always it has ended in death."

Immediately, the word began to spread and a growing murmur swelled in the night air.

Lord Rivers, his forehead furrowed in a deep frown, urged the men to dismount. He took the arm of the first messenger and led him inside. The other followed. Servants came forward to tend to the sweating, snorting horses.

As they entered the castle, the first messenger added in a loud voice over the growing din, "Her Majesty sent us from Westminster immediately after it happened — because the boy is here."

Suddenly the hubbub subsided and the eyes of all present turned to a slight, blond twelve-year-old who stood uncertainly at the far end of the main hall, his hand resting lightly on the back of a large dog.

Rivers paused, clutched at his clothing as if to make himself more presentable, then walked slowly across the room. He stopped in front of the slender boy and bowed.

"My Lord and . . ." He hesitated slightly before continuing. "My king."

Young Edward looked up at him anxiously.

" 'My king?' " His tone was uncertain. "Do you jest with me, m'Lord?"

Rivers did not respond, but his face remained so grave, the boy knew at once that something terrible had happened. He stumbled forward.

"My father — " he faltered.

How could it be? His father was only forty. Edward had never known him to be ill, and a more fun-loving, popular, party-going monarch would have been hard to find. To die when he had seemed so robust, so full of life . . .

"My king," said Rivers at last, "it happened quickly. A sudden illness. I am sorry, truly sorry. Your father was a good man and a just ruler."

Edward struggled to retain his composure. Though grief assailed him, he was aware of all the eyes upon him. It would not be seemly for the new king, however young, to lose control in public.

"I must go to the chapel and pray for him," he said, his voice strained.

A servant with a burning torch came

forward,paused for a moment, then led the boy out of the great hall to the castle chapel. Inside, Edward fell to his knees before the granite altar and bowed his head. A moment later, Rivers dropped beside him. Edward's sobs filled the cold stone room.

No one slept that night.

*   *   *

While Edward stayed in the chapel to mourn the loss of his father, watched over by his tutor Dr. John Alcock, Bishop of Rochester and Worcester, Lord Rivers sat in the great hall, pondering the boy's situation.

With the death of the king, the country could easily sink into turmoil. The House of York had wrested the crown from the House of Lancaster only after a bitter struggle. With the throne now so suddenly empty and the heir so young, the king's enemies might well attempt to install a monarch of their own choosing upon it.

To complicate matters, there was

also hostility and suspicion inside the House of York itself. The queen's family and that of the king rarely saw eye to eye on anything.

No doubt there were those who would see the king's death as an opportunity to eliminate the influence at court of the queen and her family — Lord Rivers among them.

An image of his sister grieving over her husband's death came vividly to Lord Rivers' mind. Young Edward had all her best features — the clear blue eyes, the golden hair, the high cheekbones. In point of fact, the queen was said to be the most beautiful woman in the whole of England — so beautiful that people claimed the king had married her for her looks alone. Why else, they asked, would a man of royal blood marry a mere commoner?

For Elizabeth Woodville was not a popular queen. There were those who claimed she was ruthless and ambitious, both before and after her marriage to the king. Rivers was not unaware of his sister's faults; but, to him, she did only what was necessary to protect her family in troubled times. He knew, however, that there were others who saw things differently — very differently.

The outlook for Edward could be bleak indeed if those 'others' had their way.

What, then, was the best way to protect his ward? He must watch over him carefully — even as he led him to London for his coronation, where great danger could await them both. When news of the king's death arrived, the boy had already been separated from his immediate family for several weeks. Matters of state had dictated it.

Edward IV had sent his son to Wales as his ambassador, shrewdly gambling that the boy's presence there would help to undermine the rumblings of rebellion that were being heard ever more loudly in London.

And it had indeed proved to be a

clever move. With his good looks and warm manner, the likeable Edward had quickly endeared himself to the common people.

He enjoyed appearing in public, and often waved and smiled to the crowds that came out to see him. It was not all childish exuberance, either. His ease with the populace was matched by a maturity uncommon in one so young.

In the few weeks he'd been there, Edward had grown to love Wales. But he sorely missed his family, especially his younger brother, Richard. With both their royal parents often absent or busy with affairs of state, the boys had come to rely on one another for company.

Only the presence of his uncle consoled Edward for Richard's absence. The two had quickly become fast friends.

Intelligent, skilled in mathematics, flawless in English and French and able to read and write Latin and Greek, Edward was at ease discussing any subject with his uncle. They often went for long walks together, or out riding, and passed many an hour in each other's company talking about history, warfare and the greatness of England.

As Edward grew to love Lord Rivers, his uncle grew increasingly fond of him. Not only did the boy have his mother's good looks and his father's regal bearing, but he also had something a great deal more important — the late king's intelligence and good judgement.

Perhaps most important of all, he showed an understanding far beyond his years of the role of the monarchy in the government of his country.

"A king," he said once to Lord Rivers, "should be the hope and refuge of his people as well as their sovereign ruler."

He seemed to have the wisdom of one twice his age, and Rivers was confident that with good advice and training, Edward would make a fine monarch — if only he would be given the chance.

Rivers' only worry for him before the

king's death had been that perhaps the boy's ideals were a little *too* high for the daily power struggles that were so much a part of a monarch's life.

Still, Rivers had decided, it was better to start out that way than be solely concerned with power and position from the beginning. No doubt experience would soon temper the boy's ideals where necessary.

Meanwhile, it was time for action. They must travel together to London so that Edward could be crowned as quickly as possible. There they would stay until the arrival of summer. Then Lord Rivers would accompany the boy-king back to Ludlow, returning to London with him in the fall.

They had only to await word from the capital before beginning their journey.

Lord Rivers stood and shook off the doubts which nagged him. It was time to check on his ward.

*   *   *

At dawn, a leaden sky reflected the grief at Ludlow.

With Dr. Alcock's help, Rivers had finally convinced Edward to go to his sleeping place only as the servants began to light the morning's fires.

But Edward had not rested. An image of two small boys and a bearded, laughing man haunted him. The man, his father, had an arm around each of his sons — Edward and his younger brother Richard.

The two boys, so close themselves, had worshipped their father.

The young king tossed and turned in his large, soft bed, crying until no more tears would come. Then, sleepless and scared, he lay awake and fretted — not only over the loss of his father, but also over the new role that awaited him. King of England at twelve! He felt so unprepared.

Finally, as the last traces of darkness disappeared, Edward left his bed and walked to the great hall. Rivers stood as the boy approached.

"Good morning, m'Lord," he said. "Did you sleep?"

"No, I was thinking of my father and all that his passing means."

"I too," Rivers replied.

Edward was silent.

"Your Majesty . . ."

Rivers' voice trailed off.

To Edward, the title sounded unnatural still, but he answered promptly.

"Yes?"

He hoped his tone was at least a little regal, or imperious, or however a king should sound.

"Your Grace, there is so much to do. And it must be done soon."

Rivers chose his words carefully.

"I know," said Edward.

"You will have to go to London to mourn your father and be crowned Edward V. I have sent my riders for news. They will be gone for a week at least. The two who came last night were sent in such haste that they were not able to tell me all I need to know."

"My mother," said Edward. "Did they bring a message from my mother? Where is she now?"

"There was no message," replied Rivers. "Perhaps there was no time."

* * *

Several days later, the message finally arrived.

In it, the queen sent word that she was in no danger and that she longed for Edward to join her and young Richard at Westminster Castle. She said the king had been laid to rest and the period of official mourning had begun — and would not end until after the new king arrived in London.

When he'd finished reading the queen's missive, Lord Rivers sighed quietly with relief. But then the messenger handed him a second note. Lord Rivers read it through quickly — and once more was filled with disquiet.

In the late king's will, the second

message informed him, King Edward had named his brother, Richard of Gloucester, Royal Protector to his son.

Rivers knew he had always been loyal to his sovereign. Was he not the least troublesome of his sister's relatives? Was it not the king himself who had appointed him to raise young Edward, and was it not common knowledge that he was doing a fine job? Why, then, deprive him of a responsibility that he had come to cherish and take great pride in?

Rivers did not need to be told the answer. While he was alive, the king had been just as wary as everyone else of the influence his wife's family constantly tried to exert. No doubt this was his way of counteracting that influence after his death.

Still, Lord Rivers was deeply disappointed. The youngster had been happy in Wales under his care and protection. He affirmed that happiness almost every day. Why disrupt the boy's life any more than was already necessary?

Yet the royal command had to be obeyed. Edward would have to be taken to London — to his mother and brother — and placed under the care of his uncle, the Protector, a man who was almost a stranger to him.

*   *   *

The days that followed crackled with activity.

Preparations for the journey began at dawn each day and continued until well past sunset. Rivers seemed to be everywhere — giving orders, encouraging, threatening, even laughing occasionally with the servants who were doing their utmost to ensure that the journey would go as smoothly as possible.

Provisions were laid aside. Horses that had been allowed to roam were tethered and combed. Blankets were stockpiled and clothes were washed, sorted, and placed in readiness.

Edward helped where he could, but

much of his time was taken up listening to advice concerning the duties that awaited him as England's king. Rivers coached him as best he could, but always in the forefront of his mind was the awareness that his job as the boy's guardian was almost over. At times he could not help being preoccupied with his deliberations over Richard, Duke of Gloucester, the new Royal Protector.

The man was a military leader, and had acted as a loyal and devoted servant to his brother the king. He had been sent to Scotland to keep down the threat of rebellion there and had performed the task admirably.

No, Rivers had no doubts as to Richard's qualities as a soldier. Certainly the man was brave, but was battlefield courage the best qualification for a young king's advisor? As far as Rivers was concerned, Richard was a soldier first and a statesman a distant second.

Young Edward was intelligent, but he would need guidance, and inevitably would make mistakes. It was doubtful if Richard was the best man to help him avoid those mistakes.

Still more troubling to Lord Rivers was his assessment of Richard's character. For all the duke's undeniable strengths, he was not a man Earl Rivers trusted. He had heard others voice suspicions as to Richard's true ambitions and he himself suspected his brother-in-law was not as loyal as he liked to appear. Now that his brother the king was dead, would Richard see the crown as yet another trophy to do battle for and win?

* * *

Lord Rivers kept his misgivings to himself, even when Edward noticed his pensive mood and asked if there was anything wrong.

"No, my little king," he answered, putting an arm around Edward's shoulders. "Everything is fine."

"Then tell me more about my duties," the boy persisted. "I want to serve my people well, yet even now I am not at all sure how to go about it."

"Well, Your Highness, you must strive to be fair, but you must be strong, too," counselled Rivers, his mind still half on the prospect of turning the young king over to a man he didn't trust.

"The Council will not respect you if you seem to waver or doubt your own mind."

"But surely I must give all a fair hearing?" said Edward. "I want to be a good king."

Rivers paused before responding.

"Kings are made of more than goodness," he said at last. "And how much of goodness can they do if they cannot hold on to the power entrusted to them? You must learn to handle people, Your Grace, if you would keep your crown."

"Keep my crown?" said Edward. "But how much of my time will I devote to keeping my crown, and how much will I have to give to my country?"

"The two," said Rivers reluctantly,

"are very closely bound. As you will no doubt discover."

"Until such time as I discover it," Edward rejoined with spirit, "I choose to ignore it. Now teach me all you know of governance, uncle, for I want to lead my people into a new age if I can."

Chapter 2

At last the time for departure was at hand.

Edward walked through the castle and bid farewell to the servants who had treated him so well while he was there. Then he hugged his favourite dog, climbed on the horse that was saddled for him and joined the company of the two thousand men who would ride with him. The journey to London had begun.

The ride was a difficult one. There were large tracts of forest to be crossed, forbidding swamplands and streams in spring flood. The road was little more than a trail, poorly planned, winding, muddy and long.

Yet Edward's spirits were high. He loved horses and enjoyed riding. He often galloped ahead of the others so that he could feel the wind in his face and hair.

The terrain was not unfamiliar to him, since they were traversing the same route that had brought him to Ludlow such an unexpectedly short time before.

The procession moved slowly across central England, passing through many towns and villages — some so tiny that they were little more than a few houses grouped together, others crowded with churches, inns, houses and shops, all built around a central square.

When he was not racing ahead on his own, the young king generally rode with Lord Rivers. He had so many questions to ask. But his uncle seemed withdrawn, almost taciturn, even more so than he had been the last days before their departure. Edward asked again and again what troubled him, but Lord Rivers continued to deny any cause for concern.

Four days after they left Ludlow, two horsemen thundered into the midst of the royal party. Their horses were soaked with sweat, mud-spattered and exhausted. Whatever the news, the two had wasted little time in bringing it.

"Greetings from Richard, Earl of Gloucester," said the first rider breathlessly as he reigned in beside Rivers. "Our master has sent us to find you. He is on his way to London, as you are. He wishes to join you so that together you can take the king to the city. He bids you pause at Stony Stratford and await him there."

"But why does he make such an odd request? Can he not join up with us on the outskirts of London itself?" asked Rivers.

"My Lord, we have been entrusted with the message. We do not know the reason for it. We now request your reply and your hospitality. We will take your answer with us in the morning after our horses have rested."

* * *

That night while Edward slept, Rivers and two of his most trusted advisors sat in front of the hearth at the village inn discussing the significance of the Earl of Gloucester's request.

"I do not know Richard well," Rivers said after a time, "but I am afraid there may be more to this than would appear. There is no reason for him to ride with us. He could just as easily join us in London."

"There are those who maintain the Protector wants the crown for himself, your Lordship," put in one of the advisors. "And there are others who say his fear of the Woodvilles is so great he would stop at nothing to protect himself."

That night as the last candle was doused, Lord Rivers was sure of only one thing. Whatever else might happen at Stony Stratford, his own relationship with the young king was going to come to an end even sooner than he had expected.

*　*　*

Late in the afternoon of the following day, the king's company rode into the market town of Stony Stratford, banners flying.

Waiting to greet them were Richard of Gloucester and the Duke of Buckingham — and over nine hundred men-at-arms.

The last rays of the sinking sun swept across the market square as Edward rode into it. Abruptly the hubbub subsided, the men slid from their horses and all eyes turned towards the boy.

Edward scanned the gathering and at last his eyes came to rest on the Protector.

Richard was shorter than Edward remembered, but with such a fierce look about him that his small stature seemed insignificant. He looked older than his thirty years, too, and his overall demeanour reminded Edward of ugly things he had heard said about his uncle.

But, looking at him, Edward could see that such stories were false. The man standing before him had no hideous hunchback or withered arm, and there was no permanent sneer on his face, or dribble on his chin. Rather, the stocky body stood ramrod straight, the facial muscles set and controlled. Yet Edward could see how rumours might begin. There was something frightening lurking deep in the narrowed eyes, and in the hard line of Richard's thin lips.

Despite himself, the young boy recoiled slightly.

Then Richard removed his headgear, strode to where Edward still sat on his horse, fell to his knees, and pledged his loyalty to his sovereign.

The tension of the moment was suddenly broken. Richard rose to his feet and the assembled throng broke into cheers of *God save the king!*

As the cheers echoed in the nearby streets like thunderclaps after a hot, humid day, Edward took his uncle's hand in his.

* * *

That evening, Gloucester, Buckingham, Rivers and a handful of other noblemen met. Edward was not at the meeting.

Indeed, he knew nothing about it. He had retired early to a feather bed in the local manor. The wealthy owner had been happy to give up his sleeping quarters for his king.

While he slept, Edward's future was discussed.

"My friends," Richard said to the group before him, "we are all here for the same reason. Our young king must be taken to his throne. We know he will need both guidance and help. As Protector, I intend to see that he is given that help. Henceforth, he will be in my care."

Rivers remained silent, wondering what would come next.

"I have been appointed by our late sovereign to guard and protect Edward from all harmful influences, no matter what their source," Richard continued pointedly, "and I intend to do just that. The boy is undisciplined and spoiled.He needs to be shown the error of his ways and taught self control if he is ever to learn how to wear the crown fittingly. He must be held in check; trained; not allowed to do whatever he wants."

Rivers' face grew red and he gripped the table in front of him. What treachery was this? What was the man up to?

"I take my new responsibilities very seriously," Richard continued, his eyes glittering as he stared stonily at Lord Rivers.

"I won't let the boy run wild as he did in Wales. I will teach him — "

Rivers rose to his feet, his face ashen, his whole body shaking.

"That's a lie," he shouted. "The boy was well looked after in Wales . . . he is not wild . . . he has been given good and careful guidance . . . he is not undisciplined . . . he is not spoiled . . . he will make a fine ruler."

The words poured out, jumbled on top of each other, louder and louder.

"Just who do you think you are?" Lord Rivers sputtered. "Exactly who do you think you *are*?"

"I know who I am," Gloucester snapped back. "I am the Protector to the king. Take your seat and heed my words!"

"I will not take my seat," Rivers shouted. "I love that boy dearly."

"So do I. More importantly, he is now in my charge — not yours."

"Unfortunately, that is so," Rivers thundered, "but I'll not sit idly by and watch you destroy him."

"Destroy him?" Richard shouted. "Explain yourself, my Lord, and take care how you go about it!"

"You don't know the boy at all. You will ruin him with your soldier's discipline and brutishness. He will be miserable in your charge. He is a fine, sensitive, intelligent young man. I helped raise him, and I know him."

"And now your time with him is over," Richard barked. "Understand that you are not in charge any more. It would be better for all if you were to leave now."

"What?" bellowed Rivers. "I will not

be ushered out like this! I shall remain with the boy. *You* leave!"

Richard nodded to two soldiers at the back of the room.

"You *will* go," he said with an air of grim finality, "and you will go now. You forget that I am the Royal Protector. By your words you have shown yourself to be a threat to His Majesty the King. Therefore, I am placing you under arrest."

Lord Rivers gasped in astonishment, but before he could utter another word of protest, the two soldiers gripped him firmly by the arms and dragged him forcibly from the room.

* * *

"Good morning, Your Majesty!" Dr. Alcock, Edward's tutor, stood at the foot of his royal pupil's bed.

Edward sat up abruptly.

"Why are you here?" he demanded of the familiar, portly figure. "Where is Lord Rivers?"

Embarrassed, the bishop looked beyond the boy at the blank wall.

"Where is Lord Rivers?" Edward repeated. "Tell me."

"He has gone away," the Bishop said softly.

"But he can't have."

"Yes, Your Grace, he has."

"Where? Why? We were going to London. I need him with me."

"That may be, Your Majesty, but he has gone — on the orders of the Protector. See for yourself."

The boy bounded from his bed and went to the window. Out in the courtyard he saw his own pony tethered there, but the black mare belonging to Rivers was gone. Instead there were three new horses he had never seen before. Several strangers stood about.

"What is going on?" Edward snapped. "Where did Rivers go? And why? Why did Richard do this?"

His kindly old teacher stood in silence, searching his mind for answers.

Once or twice he opened his mouth to speak, but the right words would not come. Then a knock on the door distracted him.

The Duke of Gloucester stepped into the room.

When Edward saw who it was, he leapt to his feet and snapped, "Where is Lord Rivers? He is coming to London with me."

Gloucester acted as though he had not heard.

"Good morning, Your Majesty," he said in a silky tone. "Did you sleep well? I am glad to see you are almost dressed, since we will be leaving in less than an hour. Your horse is being saddled now."

"I asked you a question," Edward responded. "Where is Lord Rivers?"

His face was crimson.

Richard smiled slightly.

"He did not feel it necessary to remain with us, Your Majesty, now that you are under my care."

Edward sensed the lie behind the words.

"Of course he wanted to go with us!" he exclaimed. "What have you done with him? Where *is* he? I demand to see him — now!"

For a few seconds Richard said nothing. Then the mask of civility dropped away and he spoke.

"I sent him away," he said coldly. "He had no part in my plans for the country."

"*Your* plans?" shouted Edward. "I am your king! *I* shall decide what is to happen to our country. You are only my Protector until I am crowned. After that, I do not need you. Remember that!"

"Oh, but I am very well aware of that, Your Highness," Richard answered coolly. "May I remind *you* that you are not crowned yet."

With that, he turned on his heel and left the room.

Edward went back to the window.

"I wonder . . . is that why Rivers

35

seemed so worried?" the boy said aloud to himself, forgetting that Alcock was still in the room.

"Yes, Your Majesty, that is why."

Edward caught his breath, startled to find he was not alone. He turned to Dr. Alcock.

"*Is* it true then?" he said miserably. "Has Richard sent Lord Rivers away?"

The good bishop hesitated. How much should he tell this frightened young boy?

"Your Grace," he said finally, "I do not know precisely what has happened, but I talked to Lord Rivers many times, and he was always afraid Richard would try to take your throne. The closer we got to London, the more he worried."

His king, Alcock decided, should know the worst, if only to prepare himself for it.

"Are his fears justified?" asked Edward.

"I do not know, Your Majesty. But there are rumours that your mother fears to leave Westminster. She does not know what Gloucester may do."

"And my brother?" Edward asked.

"He is still with her and they are both safe," the teacher continued. "In truth, I am more afraid for you."

Edward said nothing. He walked to the window and looked at the spot where Rivers' horse had been tied.

Then, as tears began to run down his cheeks, he said with great dignity, "I cannot believe, even now, that my uncle Richard is capable of such treachery to his new king."

Alcock did not contradict him. When the sobbing ceased, he said only, "I will try to find out where they took Lord Rivers, if that will ease your mind. But do not be surprised if I have only limited success. Richard likely told his men to say nothing."

"Even so," said Edward, "I would like you to try."

As soon as Dr. Alcock was gone, Edward slumped into a chair by the window. He could not remember when he had felt so lonely.

Surely what his teacher had told him was not right. True, he did not know his father's brother well, but would he actually try to take away his throne? Edward just could not believe it.

Outside, he could hear the sounds of preparation for the next leg of the journey. But Edward no longer had much interest in it. He was still sitting in the same spot, half-dressed, when Dr. Alcock returned.

"I found out nothing, Your Majesty. I asked everyone who might know, but no one would talk to me. I did not see Richard. He is busy at the inn, discussing matters with his advisors. His guards would not let me near him."

"Well, *somebody* has to know," the king replied. "I'm going to ask my servants."

"I have spoken to them already," replied Alcock. "They know nothing."

There was a loud knock. Alcock opened the door.

"Your Majesty, your horse is ready. You are to come now," said a servant. "We are leaving momentarily."

Without waiting for a response, the messenger turned and left, leaving the door open wide.

"You must go," Dr. Alcock advised. "If you don't, they will only carry you out. Please remember, your duty lies in London. All is not lost yet. As we go, I will seek news of Rivers."

"Please. If you could only do that," Edward begged as he got to his feet.

Minutes later, they were on their way.

Chapter 3

It was raining when the king's company left Stony Stratford, and Edward's spirits were as downcast as the day. Now that Rivers was gone, the young king felt very unsure of his future.

Chilling though they were, he had no real reason to doubt his tutor's ominous warnings. But still he clung to the hope that his own father's brother — his very uncle, who had known him since he was born — intended him no harm. Just what kind of man was Richard of Gloucester, anyway, he wondered? Could he really be as unpleasant — even as evil — as he seemed?

Edward's only memories of him were in terms of his father's passing comments. How often had he heard his father say, "Gloucester has put down the rebels again," and, "I owe my crown to Gloucester as much as to any man," all through his childhood? Surely such a loyal subject would not now try and take that same crown for himself?

As they rode along, Edward's thoughts turned to his other uncle, Lord Rivers, and their happy times together at Ludlow. He had been a wonderful companion, exacting and strict, but always ready to laugh and joke with his young ward. Where was he now?

As if in answer to his mournful question, cold rain began to run down the back of the young king's neck and seep through his woollen cape. He closed his eyes, held the reins in freezing fingers and let his little horse follow the trail unchecked.

Up hill and down, across the rolling greenery of southern England, they travelled for hour after endless hour. Gradually, as the hours in the saddle drew relentlessly on, Edward turned more and more within himself.

At length, a grey pony drew alongside, interrupting Edward's sorrowful thoughts. He turned to see Dr. Alcock riding alongside him.

The teacher spoke softly so that his words would not be overheard.

"Your Majesty, I finally found out about Rivers."

Edward's eyes brightened. Perhaps his beloved uncle would be joining them soon after all.

"Yes?" he said eagerly.

"He is alive, but may not be for long. They are taking him — "

"He's going to be *killed*?" Edward interrupted in alarm.

"Perhaps."

The teacher looked down.

"But why?" the boy asked. "He's done no wrong."

"Perhaps not, but the Protector wants him out of the way. You are very fond of Lord Rivers, and Richard knows that. He is jealous, Your Majesty, jealous and terribly ambitious."

"Great heavens," cried Edward. "Where is Lord Rivers now?"

"He is being taken north, to a castle near the Scottish border. Richard has friends there."

"But how do you know this?"

"As we were leaving Stony Stratford, I overheard two soldiers talking," explained Alcock. "They didn't know I was standing behind them. I hesitated to tell you earlier on the journey because I did not want Richard to see me talking to you. He does not want you to know of his plans for your uncle Rivers."

Abruptly, the teacher's horse dropped back.

Again the king was alone with his thoughts.

So Richard really is capable of evil deeds, he thought to himself, and I am in his power. He has made many friends in the north. They will do whatever he asks.

Edward thought about Richard helping the northerners, risking his life to suppress rebellion among the Scots.

He knew the man would not shrink from a challenge, and he could easily imagine him galloping into an enemy encampment astride his black mare, his cold eyes glittering mercilessly, his thin lips drawn into a tight line while he slashed and thrust with his sword.

"We are stopping now," murmured a voice off to one side. "Tomorrow the weather may clear for our entry into London."

Edward looked up, shaken out of his sodden reverie. The subject of his thoughts was but a few paces away.

"We will stop here, Your Majesty," Richard continued in an apparently respectful tone.

"Yes, that is good," replied Edward, doing his best to maintain a pretense of civility. "I am wet and cold, and also very tired."

*   *   *

The next morning, the Protector came to Edward's side, put his hand on the boy's shoulder and asked in a surprisingly friendly tone, "Did you sleep well, Your Highness?"

"Why, yes, thank you. Yes, I did," Edward replied hesitatingly. "And you?"

Gloucester nodded and smiled.

The warmth of the greeting was confusing. It seemed genuine enough.

Edward paused, then asked, "When will we be in London?"

"In about two hours," answered the Protector. "You will ride at the head of the column so that the people can see their new king. I will ride behind you."

Two servants came forward, both carrying large wicker baskets.

"I have arranged for you to wear new clothing," Richard continued. "You must look like a king now. The people want to see bright colours. The moment you are ready, we will leave."

He walked away.

Soon Edward sat resplendent on his horse, garbed in fresh new clothes. Over them he wore a purple, gold-trimmed cloak that fell from his shoulders in a regal sweep onto his horse's bright red saddle blanket. The animal's coat shone in the brilliant sun of a cloudless morning.

Richard looked equally grand in a gleaming white robe, the sword on his belt reflecting the sunlight.

When they rode into the city itself, he sat straight and proud in the saddle, waving and smiling at the assembled throngs lining the street.

Many pointed to him and murmured excitedly, convinced he was the king.

The parade wound through the narrow streets, past hundreds of ancient, smoke-stained buildings. Street urchins ran beside the horses and toothless beggars stretched their hands towards the riders, hoping these rich men might toss a coin or two in their direction. People poured from their shops as the procession passed, eager to witness this rare and exciting event.

As he moved slowly through the winding streets, Edward examined the crowd in detail. Most of the people, he knew, were poor and homeless. Many were also hungry. Few would live to an old age. Yet they all seemed happy. They waved, smiled and cheered as the riders went by.

They are happy to see their king, Edward thought to himself, touched by their devotion. If the good Lord grants me a chance to rule, I will not forget them.

A little further on, Gloucester caught Edward's attention with a wave of his arm. He was pointing towards the river and trying to be heard above the din.

"We will go down to the river bank," he shouted, "and from there, by barge to the Tower."

The Tower!

Edward stiffened in the saddle. While it was true that princes often prepared for their coronations in the Royal Apartments of the Tower of London, he had fully expected to go straight to his mother and brother at Westminster Castle.

He slapped his horse's flank and the animal trotted to the Protector's side.

"Why are you taking me to the Tower?" he asked apprehensively.

Gloucester looked into the distance without answering.

Edward repeated his question.

"Because you will be safe there," answered Gloucester finally, "and because I need to know where you are at all times. There are those, Your Majesty, who would take away your crown. As your Protector, it is my duty to see that they do not succeed."

The words sounded sincere, but they were not the words Edward wanted to hear.

"But I want to see my mother," he insisted, "and my brother."

"You will," Gloucester replied. "At the proper time."

He looked at the crowds and waved, deliberately turning from the king.

For one crazy moment, Edward thought of spurring his horse to a gallop — away from Richard, away from the river bank, away from the Tower. But there was nowhere to run to.

When the they arrived at the river's edge, the royal barge was already there waiting for them. Several smaller vessels bobbed along the shoreline and others lay at anchor in midstream.

All of them looked drab beside the splendour of the king's vessel, but Edward paid no attention.

He was overwhelmed with disappointment at not being taken to his mother and brother — and dismay at being lodged in the impregnable fortress that was the Tower.

He slid from his horse and settled quickly onto the same cushions his father had used when he journeyed by water. Once seated, the boy had to fight to hold back the tears.

Now indeed he began to know how cruel his uncle could be!

The trip down the Thames seemed to take forever. Hordes of people lined the banks of the river, shouting and straining for a glimpse of their sovereign.

"God save the king!" cried a man with a raucous voice on the nearer shore.

"God save the king!" echoed a thousand others.

Edward stood up. He tried without success to smile, but did manage to wave to his subjects. The wave set off a new frenzy of shouting.

"Hurrah for the king!" yelled a youth perched on a tree limb above the water.

"Hurrah for the king!" others shouted in response.

"Long live King Edward!" the same fellow roared at the top of his voice. "Long live King Ed — "

The joyous shout was abruptly interrupted when the limb suddenly dipped under the weight of two more spectators.

For a frozen moment the three youths clung to their fragile perch. Then the branch broke, plunging its occupants into the water.

The crowd roared with laughter.

Edward watched, but even the sudden drenching of the three failed to produce a smile.

The flotilla moved on.

At last it arrived at the stone steps leading up from the river to the edge of the foul-smelling moat.

Behind the moat was the five-hundred-year-old complex known as the Tower of London.

Edward looked distastefully up at the collection of massive stone structures. He had never liked the place — it had always seemed hostile and unfriendly. Though the buildings included the Royal Apartments as well as a zoo, council chambers and chapels, the overall impression was forbidding.

Important prisoners were often held within its walls, and public beheadings were a frequent occurrence in the open areas.

Twelve stone and flint towers loomed from the thick brick wall that surrounded the grounds. To step through the forbidding gates — and away from the longed-for embrace of his mother and brother — was terrifying.

The young king shivered as he prepared to enter.

Chapter 4

Soldiers lined the ramparts and watched as Edward stepped from the barge and passed into the grounds of the Tower. He climbed a dozen or so slime-covered steps and was steered through the great arch of the Garden Tower. Armed guards stood on either side, most of them seeing their boy-king for the first time.

Suddenly someone cackled, "Long live the king!"

A toothless hag stood just inside the gates.

"Long live the king," she repeated, grinning insanely.

A crowd of layabouts, beggars and river urchins quickly gathered, crowding close to Edward and gaping at him in open-mouthed silence.

They pressed closer, brushing up against him, reaching out tentative fingers to touch him. There was something too fervent, too desperate, in their zeal. For the first time, Edward was afraid of his subjects.

He could not help being revolted by the stench, too. The smell of sweat-stained clothes and unwashed bodies seemed to come in waves, each more sickening than the one before it.

Much to Edward's relief, the soldiers pushed the crowd aside and led him on to the group of buildings known as the Royal Apartments.

There, the young king was shown to his room by a member of his escort.

Before he closed the door, the guard bowed deferentially and said, "Lord Gloucester says you will reside here until your coronation, Your Majesty. There are servants to wait on you. Preparations for the ceremony will be underway soon."

Edward nodded but did not reply.

After the soldier withdrew, Edward looked about him curiously. The granite stone room had a high, vaulted ceiling and a huge fireplace. By one wall there was a large bed. A table and three or four stools stood in the recesses by the windows.

Edward looked out of a window on what he judged to be the side facing the river, but all he saw in front of him were walls and the cobblestoned entranceway to the Tower. Off to one side were the slimy steps he had just climbed.

He walked to the unlit fireplace and saw that there had not been a fire in it for some time. The room was cold, and, because of all the rain, the stone walls were covered with a film of moisture. Even the blankets on the bed felt damp.

Edward carried one of the window stools across to the fireplace and sat staring glumly at the few chunks of charcoal in the back. There was nothing else to burn.

As he sat there, he shivered involuntarily and thought back over the last few days.

What was going to happen to him now?

His mind drifted to his mother. She was actually only a short distance away. He wondered if she would visit him. But no doubt she would be afraid to leave the sanctuary of Westminster — afraid Gloucester would throw her in prison. And the same thing would apply to his poor little brother too, he guessed.

The hours passed and it began to grow dark outside. No one came, and Edward wondered if he had been forgotten. He was not particularly tired, but he was thirsty. A growling in his stomach told him he also needed food. He noticed for the first time a bowl and a pewter jug in a wall niche to one side of him. Both were empty. There was no candle.

Outside, the noises of the daylight hours grew more and more infrequent. From time to time he heard soldiers shouting and the tramp of marching feet. Occasionally he could hear snatches of conversation beneath the window over the entrance, but each time he looked out, the people he saw were strangers.

Edward felt all his doubts and fears crowd round him in the dark. He tried to rally himself.

Come now, he thought, you are in no real danger, at least not yet. Perhaps it is just so much malicious gossip. You are not a prisoner here.

As if to prove his point, he got up from the bed and tried the door.

It was locked.

Edward fell back against the wall. At that moment, there was a scraping sound outside and the door was slowly opened.

A stooped, burly man entered the room. He had a rough cloak on his back and he carried a wooden bowl.

Edward, numb with fear, watched him in silence.

The man set the bowl and a spoon on the table. He produced a candle from his pocket and a wax-encrusted holder in which to place it.

He lit the candle and mumbled something about coming back with some water.

Then he was gone.

Edward hurried to the table and found that the bowl was full of stew. Eagerly he sat down and spooned vegetables and chunks of meat into his mouth.

The food was cold, but it was filling, and to the hungry Edward it tasted very good. Just as he was draining the bowl to the last drop, the old man returned.

"Who are you?" Edward asked.

At first there was no reply. When Edward repeated the question, the man looked at the floor and muttered, "Peter."

"Why did you give me this food?"

"Have to," grunted the man, shifting awkwardly from side to side.

"Are you my servant then?" Edward continued gently.

"I am that."

He seemed to be very old — even

older than he had first appeared. His large weather-beaten face peered out anxiously at Edward from under an unruly mop of thick grey hair. His voice was low, like the rumble of faraway thunder, and when he spoke it was obvious there were only one or two teeth left in his mouth. His hands were gnarled and twisted.

"Please. Sit down with me, Peter," Edward offered, anxious for company, no matter from what quarter.

The old man hesitated, darted a sideways glance at the boy and then shuffled across the room to one of the window stools. He sat there, staring at the floor, clasping his hands.

"Do you know who I am?" asked the king.

"Yes, Master."

"Are you afraid of me?"

"I am that," Peter replied.

"But why? I won't hurt you. It seems I am a prisoner here."

Peter said nothing. Instead, he

pulled his cloak around himself, as if trying to hide behind it. He kept his eyes on the floor while his feet continued to shuffle nervously.

Edward shrugged and continued.

"I may be the king, but as long as I am here I have no power. Besides, I would never hurt you. I need you, Peter. I need you to look after me. Will you do that?"

There was a long silence. Then, without looking up, Peter spoke.

"Yes, Master, I'd like that."

"Well, thank you, Peter," Edward's voice trembled a little with emotion. "I am glad you want to serve me."

He crossed the room and pressed a small coin into the old man's hand. Peter shrank farther into his cloak.

Edward returned to his own seat and carried on talking.

"I have never been here as a prisoner before, so I don't know what to expect. You can show me what I must do. You know about this place."

"Yes, Master. May I go now?"

Peter got to his feet and shuffled to the door.

Mumbling an embarrassed "Good night, Your Highness," he opened the door and was gone.

The king turned to his bed.

* * *

Edward fell asleep almost as soon as he burrowed under the coarse blankets, tired out from the events of the last few days. He did not stir again until awakened by the hot rays of the sun shining on his face.

He was still in bed when Peter brought Dr. Alcock into the room.

When Edward saw his teacher, he bounded to his feet, bursting with questions.

"Good morning, Your Grace," said his teacher. "How did you sleep?"

"Well," Edward replied. "I was very tired. But why are you here? Are you here to teach me? Can I go out now? How long do I have to stay here?"

"Patience, patience, my little king. You will have to learn patience. I cannot answer your questions. It seems no one can except the Protector, and he has not told anyone of his plans. Preparations should be underway for your coronation, Your Highness, but I am not sure of . . . "

His voice trailed off.

"Not sure of what?" demanded Edward.

"Not sure of what the Protector has in mind," Dr. Alcock replied reluctantly. "He says you can come and go as you please within the Tower complex, but he has ordered the guards not to let you leave the grounds. And apart from the old man here, only I can visit you."

"*I* am the king," Edward wailed desperately. "It is not up to my uncle to say where I may or may not go."

"That is true," his tutor sighed. "But . . . "

"Go on," urged Edward. "Please. You must tell me all you know. You must not treat me like a child any longer. I cannot be king if I still think like a child."

"I am not sure that learning of the intrigues of adults helps you," responded Dr. Alcock kindly. "Consider your reaction to the news of Lord Rivers that I brought you."

"But how can I govern without knowing these things?" countered Edward. "If God grants me a chance to rule England, I must understand. Go on."

"As you wish," sighed Dr. Alcock. He turned to the old servant. "You may leave us," he said.

"Oh, Peter can stay," put in the young king. "He has my trust."

"Very well, Your Highness. Your uncle is a strong-willed and avaricious man, and there are those who, for their own reasons, would capitalize on his greed to persuade him to take the throne for himself. They are confident of his acceptability here because he is almost a stranger in this part of the country. What the people do not know about a man, they will not hold against him. It is only in the north that he is well known."

"But I am the king's son," Edward interjected. "I am heir to the throne."

"I know that," Alcock went on, "and so do the people. But many do not want a boy-king because they worry about who would rule in your place until you are grown. Richard is the king's brother and an adult. That is another reason why they may support him."

"And if all this is true, what is to become of me?" Edward asked plaintively.

"You are to be lodged here for the present," said Alcock. "I shall visit you as often as possible. Perhaps we should continue with your schooling. Working on your mathematics would certainly help you forget about the restrictions on your freedom."

Alcock's attempt at humour did little to cheer the young king.

"Mathematics won't help me see my mother and brother," he sighed. "I thought when I was brought to London I would be with them."

"So did I," said Alcock, "but the Protector had decided otherwise."

"Do you think that perhaps I could visit them, just for a little while?" asked Edward. "I would even go with soldiers to guard me and bring me back. Would my uncle allow that, do you think?"

"I doubt it," Alcock responded, "but I could ask. Would you like that?"

"Oh, yes, I would," said Edward, "and as soon as possible. I miss them terribly."

"I will be talking to the Protector tomorrow. Is there anything else?"

Edward hesitated, his face hardening.

"Yes. Ask him for news of Lord Rivers. Also, tell Gloucester I want to see him personally."

"I will do that, Your Majesty, but you must not count on him answering your summons."

"Tell him I *insist*," replied the king.

Alcock promised to deliver the message. Then he and Peter left the room, leaving the door open behind them.

Chapter 5

Edward stared at the open door for several seconds. Then he walked to a window and looked out at the spring sunshine. Two soldiers were standing below, enjoying the warmth of the morning. One of them glanced upwards and was startled to see that he was being watched. He nudged the man with him, who turned in Edward's direction.

The boy did not react at first, but then he nodded and smiled. Both men waved and smiled in return. Edward stepped back from the window, relieved that not all the soldiers were as stern and forbidding as those he had seen on his arrival.

He had a drink from a water jug Peter had left, and decided that now was the time to begin exploring his surroundings.

Just as he was about to leave the room, Peter arrived with a bowl of porridge, a shy toothless grin on his face.

"You look happy," said Edward, pleased to see another cheerful face.

The old man mumbled incoherently.

"Tell me what is making you happy," said the boy.

Silence.

"Come on, Peter, tell me," Edward coaxed.

The servant stepped back and smiled again, his eyes crinkling at the corners.

"Guide, Your Grace," he said. "Just me."

Edward was not sure what he meant.

"Just me," the old man repeated proudly, pointing to his chest. "I been here longer than any. I knows the Tower like my own home. I been appointed your guide. Just me. I can show you places you never seen."

Now the boy understood.

"Well, that *is* good. I am quite familiar with some parts of the Tower, but there are others I have only heard tell of. I feel very honoured to be shown around by such an expert guide."

Peter beamed with undisguised delight.

As soon as he had eaten his porridge, Edward followed the old man down the steps from the Royal Apartments. It cheered him a little that a tour had been arranged. Surely it was not likely that a tour would be given to a prisoner? Perhaps his uncle's intentions were not as black as they appeared.

It was a slim hope, but better than none at all.

When they entered the courtyard, a crowd gathered almost immediately. Many stared at Edward. A few came close, and one or two even touched him, as if to convince themselves that he was real.

This time Edward was not as frightened as he had been before.

Many in the gathering worked within the Tower walls. Some were visiting and a few were present because, like the crowd the day before, they had nowhere else to go. Everybody seemed to be awed by the young king, and they all tagged along as Peter began his tour. "Begging pardon, Your Highness, but do you want me to tell you about the Tower?" Peter asked.

"As you wish," said Edward.

He was surprised that Peter was so willing to talk. The old man was getting quite garrulous.

"Please. Go ahead," the boy invited. "Tell me all you know."

"Well, Your Grace," Peter began, warming to his task. "These here fortifications were first built to protect England from rebellion and terrible evils like that. But as it turns out, and if Your Majesty don't mind me saying so, other evils just as terrible have been done right here within these very walls — things most folks know nothing of."

"Evils done? What evils? And done to whom?" Edward asked, his eyes wide.

"Traitors, Your Majesty. Traitors and other wicked people. People such as them are brought here and thrown into dungeons deep beneath our feet and left to rot, year after year — that is, if the torture don't kill them."

"Torture?"

"Yes, torture, Your Highness, to make them tell the truth," Peter said. Then he added solemnly, "Ah, but who knows what kind of truth they tell just to stop the hurting?"

The old servant suddenly fell silent, frightened by his own boldness.

Edward said nothing, so Peter resumed, his courage returning.

"Your Majesty, how be it if we go see them dungeons now? There are some there as have never seen you. They have been there since before you was born."

Edward nodded mutely, so without further ado, Peter led the way down a set of narrow, wet, winding stone stairs. Edward followed slowly. He knew that his father had taken a hard line with rebels. He knew also that part of the Tower of London served a prison. But torture he had not heard about.

Part of him wanted to run away, but another part — the part of him that needed to know all there was to know about his realm — propelled him forward.

Cautiously, Edward continued to descend the dank smelly stairwell, helped a little by the light of candles flickering in wall niches. Finally they arrived at the bottom.

"There are many here, Your Grace," Peter announced, pointing through heavy metal bars into an alcove where several men lay on the floor.

For a few seconds, the boy saw nothing in the darkness. Then slowly the shadows settled into recognizable shapes and his heart beat thickly against his chest. As he gasped for air, he felt as though he were drowning in blood: his own and that of the wretched prisoners who lay silently before him, covered in filth and open sores, their hair long and bedraggled.

Edward clutched the bars and could not look away.

At length, Peter led him on. The boy was ready to turn back, but his servant was too caught up in the tour to realize it. Innocent in his enthusiasm and long used to the Tower's worst sights and sounds, he took the young king straight to the true chamber of horrors, the frightful place where prisoners were tortured.

Inmates hung from the stone walls by their wrists, their skin so taut against their ribs it looked as if the bones might break the flesh at any moment. One man appeared dead, but opened his eyes at Peter's touch.

Edward thought he might be sick. What crime could possibly deserve such punishment? What good could this do? How could his father have let this happen?

When I am king, the boy resolved, I will put an end to this horror.

But the worst was yet to come.

Peter led the way to what looked like a metal bed with rollers at either end, plus one in the middle.

"Look at this, Your Highness," said Peter.

"What is it? What do they do with it?" Edward asked in horror.

"It is called the rack, Your Grace. Them as refuses to confess get laid on here, and then their ankles and wrists are tied with ropes to them rollers at the ends. When the victim is secured, the rollers are turned and the ropes tighten. The prisoner is stretched, Your Majesty, very, very slowly. Sometimes they never do confess, and their bodies are stretched until they die. I seen it once. It weren't nice."

"Take me somewhere else, Peter," Edward begged. "I've seen enough of this."

Peter looked at him and grinned his

toothless grin before leading him on to the armoury where the weapons of war were stored.

Edward still felt shaky, and barely listened as Peter described the lances, swords, pikes, suits of armour and crossbows piled in heaps around them.

Because the Tower had been an armed garrison for almost five hundred years, some of these weapons were ancient. Others were more modern. All were deadly.

Though Edward knew that the central White Tower and the walls that surrounded it were probably the strongest fortification in the land, he was still surprised at the size of the armoury.

Once outside again, Peter related a story that involved another uncle of Edward's, a man named George, Duke of Clarence.

"He made enemies, he did," Peter confided. "Forgive me for saying it, Your Grace, but he done a lot of terrible things. One time he had two servants killed. *His* servants. And he didn't even give them no trial. So he was put on trial himself, and was sentenced to death for murder. But being a nobleman and all, he was allowed to choose his own manner of dying. You will never guess what manner of death he chose, Your Majesty."

Edward blanched.

"No, I suppose I never will," he said reluctantly. "Tell me."

"He was partial to the drink, you see, so he chose to drink himself to death. Sure enough, they tied his hands and feet and put him in a huge barrel of wine" — Peter paused for a moment to cackle delightedly — "and then they put the top on the barrel. Then he drank and drank until he drowned."

Peter slapped his thighs and roared with laughter.

Edward smiled at the old man's laughter and waited until it had subsided before asking to see something else — something pleasant.

"I know the very thing, Your Grace,"

Peter said, wiping his eyes with grimy knuckles as he tried to regain his composure. "You'll like this."

He led the way to the zoo, a small collection of animals kept for the entertainment of visitors to the Tower. Its oldest inhabitant was a polar bear called Jocko, who caught his own food from the river. In addition, there were two lions and two leopards, a small number of birds and several monkeys.

Judging from the crowd gathered around the monkey cages, these lively little creatures were the most popular attraction. Edward stepped closer.

Two small, tan-coloured monkeys were putting on a show. One swung from a perch high up in the cage, then suddenly leapt across the enclosure and tried to knock its mate from a narrow wooden bar near the front. It did this over and over again. But each time it jumped, its mate dodged out of range, then turned to the crowd and bowed. As the spectators applauded, Edward found himself laughing for the first time that morning.

As luck would have it, Peter and Edward arrived just as the zoo keeper was getting Jocko ready to go and catch his supper.

The keeper entered Jocko's cage and carefully slipped a leather collar with a harness attached around the animal's neck. A length of rope was tied to the harness. With the rope in his hand, the keeper opened the door and he and Jocko walked out of the cage.

Edward stepped forward.

"Could I pet him?" he asked the keeper.

The man nodded.

"He is a gentle beast," he said.

"Here, Jocko. Here, Jocko."

The king moved closer to the bear. The animal turned and waited.

"His hair is so soft," the boy laughed. "And I love his little ears."

He touched them gently. Peter grinned.

Then the keeper led the way across the yards, with Jocko waddling along behind.

At the Tower entrance, the soldiers opened the gates for the pair to pass. When they reached the river, the bear waded in to fish.

On later occasions, Edward watched from the Tower walls as the bear caught and ate his fill before being led back to his cage. In the midst of uncertainty, he found the daily ritual strangely reassuring.

Chapter 6

About a week after his arrival in the Tower, Edward was awakened one morning by Dr. Alcock.

"I have news from the Protector, Your Majesty," he said as soon as the boy was sitting up. "He says to tell you that affairs of state require all his time, and that he cannot spare a moment to visit you. And, Your Highness — "

Alcock paused. It would break the boy's heart to hear what he had to say next.

"What is it, Dr. Alcock?"

"Richard says you may not visit your mother."

"I am not surprised." Edward's voice was low. "My uncle cares only for himself. That much is obvious. Is he now going to make himself king?"

"Nothing is certain, Your Majesty,"

said his tutor sadly, "but I suspect that is the case. He confers daily with Lord Buckingham and others, and has been seen publicly in various parts of the city. They say he is soon going to journey to Warwick Castle to plan his future. The trip will be another opportunity to show himself to the people. In my opinion, that is the real reason he is going."

Edward remembered Warwick Castle. It was a magnificent structure, two days' journey west of London.

Set on high ground overlooking a vast sweep of plain, the castle was owned by the Earl of Warwick and had long been a favourite retreat from the cramped and stifling surroundings of London. The country air was sweet and pure and a little stream behind the castle teemed with fish.

"Do you really think Richard cares what the people think?" Edward asked.

"Yes — insofar as he needs their support, Your Majesty."

"How much support does he have now?"

"A great deal, Your Highness. But he has one major obstacle."

"What is that?"

"You," said Alcock flatly.

Edward flinched.

"Is that how he sees me now — an obstacle?"

"Your Majesty," replied Alcock, "we cannot have two kings. Richard knows that. He also knows that your coronation is supposed to be on June 22nd. Because it is now almost the middle of May, that leaves him barely a month to act. Richard is a strong and ruthless man, Your Majesty, and I believe he will stop at nothing in order to get his way."

"You mean, he might leave me here?"

"Yes," Alcock replied. "He might do that — or he might do something worse than that."

Edward looked up.

"What do you mean?" he asked nervously.

Alcock hesitated, then at last revealed his innermost fears.

"My boy, he might have you killed," he said, his voice trembling, his kindly eyes moist.

The statement was like a blow to Edward's body. He staggered backwards under its impact and slumped down onto a stool. Tears welled in his eyes and his face lost all its colour.

"I have wanted to warn you ever since the day you came here."

Dr. Alcock was speaking softly now, but his voice was firm and not at all reassuring.

"I just could not find the words. You are in grave danger, Your Grace. Do you understand me? Do you realize what I am saying?"

"Yes. Yes, I do understand," Edward replied after a time. "But what can I do? I cannot leave here and I cannot defend myself. I have no power."

"That remains to be seen," said Alcock, "but first there is something else I must tell you."

"Yes, what is it?" asked the king, his voice weary.

"I have received news of Lord Rivers."

"Oh, thank God!" cried Edward, and he jumped to his feet. "Tell me! Tell me!" he begged. "Perhaps he can suggest a plan. He would know — "

Abruptly Edward broke off, his hopes dashed by the look on Dr. Alcock's face.

"Your Majesty, I have just learned that Lord Rivers has been executed."

"No! Oh, no!" Edward wailed. "Why? He did no wrong. He was a good and kind man. He was loved by many, not just me."

Alcock put his arm around the boy's shoulders. Edward sobbed, barely hearing Alcock's explanation.

"Perhaps the Protector feared that Lord Rivers, like himself, coveted your throne," said the teacher. "Or perhaps he just did not like the fact that Rivers was your confidant. Whatever the reason, your uncle's death indicates that it is imperative that you act now.

"When I visit you tomorrow, Your Majesty, I shall endeavour to take you out of this place with me. I have arranged for a supply cart to follow me and I have persuaded your servant Peter to help.

"After I have been here, he will place you inside a coal sack and put you on the cart. The cart will take you to a house in Shropshire where I will later join you. From there we will journey to France if necessary."

The boy lifted his head.

"But would I not be deserting my country if I did that?" he asked solemnly.

"I would not suggest this course of action if I thought there was the slightest hope you would be allowed to wear your crown," was the terse reply.

* * *

Dr. Alcock remained with the king for over an hour, talking softly to him, consoling him like a father. Finally, when the boy seemed calm, the teacher bowed and left the room.

"I will come for you early in the morning," he said as he left.

Edward sat still, listening to the footfalls on the stone stairs. As the sounds died away, he became aware of an aching hollowness inside.

If only his mother were with him. He needed her arms around him to protect him, to turn the cruel world away. He knew she must also be in danger, or she would have come to him.

He wondered about his brother. Was he well? Was he happy?

Slowly, as he thought about his family, hope rose in Edward. If all went well tomorrow . . .

And perhaps it would. Dr. Alcock was a brave and clever man. Edward was suddenly excited. Was escape really so impossible? Perhaps this time tomorrow he would be free of the Tower of London, free of the burden of kingship, free to meet with his beloved family in France.

That night, as Edward finally drifted off to sleep, his last thought was of his mother's smile.

* * *

The next day, Edward rose early to finish breakfast before his teacher arrived. He was too excited to eat very much, and was soon pacing his room.

If only there were something I could do, he thought, to help the plan succeed! But all I can do is wait, and hope, and pray.

Now that Edward had accepted the possibility of escape, he was desperate to try it. He could almost feel his mother's arms around him, his brother's hand in his.

After a time, he rose to look out the window. Surely the good doctor would be here soon? What could be keeping him, anyway?

I will make myself busy, thought

Edward, so that I will stay calm. My part in this plan will be to have courage, the courage to be still and quiet and patient.

An hour went by and still Alcock did not come. The little king had done all he could to distract himself, and now again he was pacing back and forth, stopping each time at the window to peer down into the courtyard.

Outside it was raining a heavy downpour — so much a part of England in the spring that ordinarily it would have raised young Edward's spirits. Now as he watched the rivulets cascade down the windows and listened to the drumming of raindrops loud upon the roof, he could barely keep from crying out.

Once or twice he was sure he heard Alcock's step outside. But each time he went to the top of the stairs, no one was there. The day wore on and the young king became more and more distracted.

I shall go mad, thought Edward.

Finally he left his room and wandered about the Tower grounds, ignoring the rain. Even the antics of the monkeys in the zoo could not console him.

What had happened to Alcock? And what would happen to him now?

As he walked up the steps to his room, he was sure he could hear the prisoners moaning in the dungeons below.

The rain continued, the shadows lengthened and at last the daylight turned to dusk. Outside, there were puddles of water everywhere, and high overhead masses of grey cloud swirled around the heavens. Two soldiers at the gate huddled against the wall in a futile attempt to keep dry. No one moved. No one came to the Tower.

Darkness had fallen by the time Peter arrived with the evening meal. Edward was still sitting by a window, listening to the rain, his heart heavy and his thoughts full of despair. Even being reminded by Peter's presence that there were men willing to put themselves at great risk for his sake did not cheer him.

Peter set the meal in front of the boy

and urged him to eat. When Edward did not react, the servant spoke to him again in the brusque yet familiar manner that friends use with each other.

"You must eat, Your Grace," said the old man. "You need to keep up your strength. He might come tomorrow."

Peter looked up.

"Yes, I suppose he might," he agreed. "But why did he not come today?"

"That I do not know, Your Highness," answered the old man sadly. "But you must eat. Mayhap he was delayed. He is an important person. 'Tis possible he had to go elsewhere at a moment's notice, and will come tomorrow."

There was logic in the servant's words, and Edward allowed himself to be soothed by them. He ate and retired for the night.

* * *

Alcock did not come the next day, or the day after that. Edward waited fretfully, sitting beside the window, watching the Tower entrance.

For the first two days, Edward ate what Peter put before him, but as the days wore on, he began to consume less and less. By the time a week had passed, he was taking barely any nourishment at all.

"I am too tired, Peter," was all he would say when his servant urged him to eat.

Peter clucked and fussed like a mother hen.

After a time, the boy began to remain in bed for hours, sometimes sleeping, sometimes staring listlessly at the ceiling overhead.

Then one day Peter was called to the front gate to pick up a note addressed to Edward. The servant carried the message to his king and waited for the boy to read it.

The note was short, blunt — and devastating. It informed the king that Dr. Alcock, his respected tutor, was dead.

Chapter 7

Edward read the words again and again, hoping that somehow they would change. Finally, he threw the note down and buried his face in his pillow.

Peter picked up the paper and left the room. He had no idea what the marks on the page said, but it was not difficult to see that somehow they had hurt his young king badly — and at a time when he was already in a sadly weakened state.

Edward rarely left his bed now, and had not eaten in days. A little water was all the sustenance that had passed his lips.

Something had to be done, but what? There was no way Peter could contact the boy's mother, so in desperation he finally decided to approach the Constable of the Tower, Sir Robert Brackenbury. There was no other course of action open to him.

When he arrived at the Constable's quarters, the guard refused to let him enter.

"I will take the paper to him," he said, eyeing the note in Peter's hand, "if that is what you wish to see him about. You will go no further."

"Tell the Constable my master is sick," Peter said as he handed the guard the note, "and this made him worse."

Then he sat down on the ground to await a reply.

Several minutes passed and Peter was beginning to wonder at the delay when a tall, thin, grey-haired man came to the doorway. Sir Robert himself. He puffed on a pipe while Peter scrambled to his feet.

"You are the servant to the king?" Sir Robert asked.

"I am that," Peter answered. "Begging your pardon, Sir Robert, but His Grace is sick. The message made him worse."

"Oh, yes, the note. Bad news, I'm sorry to say," Sir Robert said casually. "Poor Alcock. Killed in a fall from his horse. Always was prone to be a little unsteady in the saddle."

Brackenbury did not seem surprised or upset by Alcock's death. He questioned Peter further.

"The king is sick you say? In what way?"

"He remains in his bed all day and will not eat."

"Go on."

"He is very weak."

Peter paused. This was the first time he had admitted his worst fears, even to himself.

"I think he is going to die."

"Does he need a doctor?" Brackenbury asked.

"I believe he does. But begging your pardon, Sir Robert, he needs his mother or his brother more. He is so lonely. It is that what's killing him."

Sir Robert narrowed his eyes.

"Why so?" he asked.

"Sir, he talks about them all the time."

Brackenbury's lips twitched.

"He misses his brother, does he?" he asked with a smile.

"Terrible bad," said Peter. "Help him, please, sir, or he will surely die."

Brackenbury was lost in thought, as if his mind had wandered off somewhere else. Abruptly, without another word to Peter, he turned and went back inside.

Puzzled, Peter waited a minute to see if Brackenbury would return. Finally he left, content that he had done all he could.

*   *   *

All the rest of that day, and all through the night that followed, the king remained in bed.

Peter stayed by his side, talking to him, doing his best to keep him comfortable, and urging him to at least drink as much water as possible.

Shortly before dawn, the servant nodded off to sleep.

He awoke with a start a short while later, just as the morning sun began to flood the room. But it was not the sunlight that had aroused him. It was the sound of a child's voice calling from the courtyard below.

Wearily Peter hauled himself to his feet and, yawning, shuffled to the window. Outside, several well-dressed men were standing about while a guard talked to a young boy. Then the men departed and the guard took the boy inside.

A minute or so later, the child climbed the stairs to the Royal Apartments alone.

The King of England had a visitor.

As soon as Peter opened the door, nine-year-old Prince Richard, Duke of York, went straight to his brother's side. He stood quietly for a moment, staring at the pallid face on the pillow.

"Brother. Brother," he cried at last. "Wake up! It's me, Richard. Wake up!"

Edward's eyes fluttered open and he gazed around as if trying to remember where he was. When his eyes began to close again, Richard nudged him gently and called his name once more.

And once more Edward opened his eyes. This time they focused on Peter at the end of the bed.

"You have a visitor, Your Grace," said Peter, smiling.

Edward stirred and raised his head, attempting to sit up. Finally he recognized his brother.

"Richard!" he cried weakly, his eyes wide with joy. "Is it really you?"

Edward nodded and held out his hand and his younger brother clasped it in his own.

"What's the matter, brother?" asked Richard. "Are you sick? Why are you in bed? It's morning, you know, and I have come to be with you."

At these words, the king flinched

strangely. He asked Richard to repeat what he had said.

"I am going to stay with you here," said the young prince. "For as long as you want me."

The smile on Edward's face died.

"But who brought you here? Who gave permission?" he asked.

"I am not sure," said Richard. "Mother said a man here in the Tower said it was important that I come. I do not know who. Mother cried when I left, but she said that you needed me more than she. Are you not glad to see me?"

Edward's mind was in a whirl.

Even if my uncle contented himself with keeping me here forever, he thought, he would still have to deal with Richard. He is in line for the throne if anything happens to me. Our uncle has us where he wants us now.

"Of course I am glad to see you," he said, swallowing hard. "I am *very* glad to see you."

98

And he reached over and hugged his brother.

Peter cleared his throat, muttered something about going for food and disappeared.

When he returned, Edward was sitting on the edge of the bed holding a cup of water. For the first time in days, there was a slight smile on his face.

"I see you have brought us breakfast," he said to Peter quietly. "I think I will eat a little this morning."

"There is plenty to eat, Your Grace, but you must take just a little at first because you have not eaten for so long," Peter cautioned. "I will bring more later, if you wish it."

Edward ate a small portion of his breakfast, then asked for help in getting up. He was so unsteady on his feet he could only take a few steps before had to lie down again. Richard helped him, chatting non-stop all the while.

Listening to his brother was very comforting to Edward. There was something so commonplace about being with Richard that, despite their terrible circumstances, he began to smile in earnest.

Chapter 8

Over the next few days, Edward thought about telling his brother the truth of their situation, but could not decide if that would be the right thing to do or not. How awful it would be for carefree, light-hearted Richard to be overwhelmed with dread and fear the way he had been!

So in his indecision, Edward remained quiet on the subject and took heart in his brother's company. Each day, he grew a little stronger and more active.

Then, four days after Richard's arrival, he went to the window, looked out onto the sun-drenched courtyard and cried, "Let us go outside today!"

The date was June 19, 1483, only three days before Edward's coronation was due to take place.

As Edward dressed, he thought

about the fact that still no instructions had arrived about preparing for the occasion, but he said nothing.

Perhaps if I am not crowned it will be all for the best, he told himself. If I am not made king, then Richard may forget all about us.

He remembered Dr. Alcock saying that Gloucester was popular among the people who knew him — so perhaps he would not make a bad king.

He had also heard from Peter, rumours that Gloucester had had both himself and Richard declared illegitimate and therefore ineligible to inherit the crown. If the rumour was true, and if Gloucester's declaration as to their illegitimacy was accepted, then the brothers would pose no further threat to him.

The idea of being declared illegitimate was not pleasant — in fact it was an insult and it made Edward angry — but it did carry with it some hope.

If it saves my brother's life, I will accept it, he thought.

When he was dressed, Edward looked over at Richard, who was still trying to pull himself into his clothes.

"Come on, Richard!" he urged his brother. "I have been cooped up in here too long."

"Why must I hurry?" grumbled the younger boy. "The day has barely begun."

When Richard was finally dressed, the boys went outside together.

It was a bright sunny day and Edward felt almost carefree as they stepped into the courtyard.

"Come and look, Richard," he said excitedly. "You will love this part of the Tower."

He raced off towards the building where the wild animals were kept, his little brother hard on his heels.

"This is my favourite part of the whole place," he said, panting, as they arrived.

Richard's eyes grew wide as he looked inside. At first he clung to the door, afraid to go farther. But when he realized these strange animals were behind bars and could not hurt him, he ran from cage to cage, shrieking with delight. Like Edward, he found the monkeys most fascinating of all.

"Edward, look, look," he cried. "Watch this one. She is hanging by her tail."

But no sooner had the king turned to look, than Richard was pointing to another monkey, and laughing so hard his brother was afraid he might choke.

The monkey he was pointing to was tiny with big eyes and an impish expression. Over and over again she tossed a stick into the air, jumped to a ledge and caught it just before it fell onto the head of her mate. Each time, she looked to Richard for approval before repeating the trick.

After a little while, she came to the front of the enclosure and stared intently at him. The young prince stepped back, disconcerted. For a moment he felt as though he were the one in the cage.

The boys were still enjoying the antics of the monkeys when the zoo keeper arrived to take Jocko the bear to catch fish in the Thames.

"Where are they going?" Richard asked as the keeper led the huge bear from its cage.

"To the river," Edward replied. "The keeper takes Jocko on a leash, but it is long enough for him to wade into the water to catch fish. It's fun to watch. We can see from the top of the wall."

Richard looked puzzled.

"Why do we have to watch from the wall? Let's just go out to the river with the keeper. He won't mind. Come on!"

Edward stood speechless as Richard ran ahead of the keeper. The guards opened the gates and the boy stepped aside to let Jocko and the keeper pass. Then he started to follow behind them.

Desperately, Edward called out, "Richard! Wait!"

Suddenly a guard ran toward Richard yelling, "You, there! Stop! You must not pass. Stop!"

He grabbed Richard by the scruff of the neck and jerked him backwards. Richard struggled in the guard's grip, but the man simply shook him like a puppy. Then the angry boy reached behind him and scratched at the guard's arm. With a howl and a curse, the guard slammed Richard down face first onto a granite flagstone.

Richard lay motionless on the ground where he'd landed and blood spread from beneath his downturned face in an ever-widening stain over the stones.

The guard wheeled around and walked away, brushing past Edward as though he was not even there.

The king rushed forward.

"Brother, brother," he cried as he

knelt beside the injured boy. "Are you all right?"

He turned Richard over, loosened the neck of his tunic, and held a handkerchief to the blood running from a gash in his brother's forehead.

Slowly Richard's eyes opened. He looked up with a mixture of astonishment and pain. His voice was hoarse when he spoke.

"What happened, brother?"

"The guard threw you down," Edward replied. "Now, don't move. Your head has a bad cut and I want to check the bleeding. Then I will help you up to bed."

"But the bear . . ."

Richard's question trailed off.

"They are at the river's edge. The guard would not let you follow."

"Why not?" came the anguished response. "Are we prisoners here, Edward?"

Edward could only nod in response.

"Why are we being kept here,

Edward?" Richard asked when the brothers had returned to their room.

He was sitting on the bed, still holding Edward's handkerchief to his forehead.

"I don't want to be a prisoner!"

Edward looked at his brother's tear-stained face and suddenly felt a good deal more than just three years older. He wished he did not have to tell Richard what he feared, wished even more that the younger boy had never been brought to the Tower.

"The Duke of Gloucester wants to be King of England, Richard," he said as gently as he could. "And he does not want us interfering with his plans."

"But you are the king, aren't you, Edward?" said his brother. "Mother said you were to be crowned king soon."

"I was to be crowned three days from now," said Edward. "But no preparations have been made. Uncle Richard has decided to make himself king instead."

"Well, if he does, will he set us free?"

"Of course he will," said Edward soothingly.

He only wished he believed it himself.

*   *   *

June 22nd came and went. Edward was not crowned, but as far as he knew, the Protector had not yet made himself king, either.

On the 23rd, after the two boys had returned from playing outside on the grounds, Peter came to them, his face lined with worry. He asked both to sit down and then slowly and painfully, he began to speak.

"Two men from the city have been to see the Constable of the Tower," he said. "The Constable called for me when they left and told me to bring a good supply of food and water to you and leave it here. When I asked why, he told me to do what I was ordered."

The old man stopped to catch his breath.

"Then he said I would not see much

more of you. He said you may not go out-side after today. You must both stay in this room all the time."

The boys listened in stunned silence. Then they bombarded Peter with questions.

"We are to be locked up in here, locked up in this room?" demanded Edward.

Peter nodded, then hung his head, as if ashamed to be the carrier of such news.

At first Richard did not understand just how serious the situation was.

"Edward," he said, "what does this mean? Can we *never* go out?"

When Edward did not respond, the little boy turned to Peter.

"Can we never go out, ever again?" he asked. "Are we to stay here until we die?"

The servant raised his head reluctantly. There were tears in his eyes.

"I do not know, my Lord," he answered. "I do not know."

The old man got up slowly, as if he were in pain.

"I must go now," he said. "And I do not know when I will be back."

After his footsteps had died away in the distance, the silence in the room was almost painful.

"What does this mean, brother?" Richard said at last.

"I am not certain, Richard, but I suspect that our uncle Richard will now make himself king."

"But why must he lock us away?"

"Because there are people who think that what he is doing is wrong. They know I am the rightful heir to the crown, not him. I suppose he thinks the fewer who see us, the better. But we must not let our spirits fall. We must try to be happy, for it may be that our days here will be few. Perhaps our uncle will have us sent out of the country soon to somewhere where no one knows our history."

But days passed and no word came to the Tower.

Finally on July 6th, Peter visited them and brought the news that Richard, Duke of Gloucester, had been crowned King Richard III.

Chapter 9

To Richard and Edward in the Tower, the hours spent in their room seemed to stretch on endlessly. There was nothing to do. The food Peter had brought ran out after a few days, and soon they were hungry as well as bored and frightened.

One morning, to take his mind off his stomach and to distract his little brother from their troubles, Edward began doing some acrobatics.

"Richard, can you do this?" he asked.

"Do what?" Richard was staring out the window, his back to the room.

"This," Edward repeated.

Richard turned to see his brother standing on his head.

"Of course I can do that. Watch!"

Richard got down on his knees, put his head and hands on the floor and tried to boost his legs into the air.

He tumbled down.

He tried a second time and failed. On his third attempt, his legs came up but he flipped head over heels and crashed onto his back. He picked himself up, red-faced and determined.

"Just watch, brother, just watch."

Again he pitched forward and somersaulted across the room, knocking a stool over in the process.

"See, I *knew* you couldn't," Edward taunted.

"I can too!" He tried again. Again he fell.

Edward teased some more.

It was too much for Richard. He lunged at his big brother, fists flying. The two boys grappled with each other, flailing around on the floor. Richard had Edward by the hair and would not let go. Because he was smaller than his brother, he thought it fair to fight any way he wished. Edward refused to give up. They were still wrestling and shouting at each other when the door opened.

"Great heavens! What are you boys doing, fighting like this?" laughed Peter as he carried food and water into the room. "Are you having a war?"

The boys scrambled to their feet, embarrassed at being caught fighting, but wildly happy to see their old servant again. Edward blushed and attempted to adjust his tunic. Richard recovered first.

"I beat him, Peter," the younger boy boasted. "You should have *seen* me!"

The servant chortled, set food down on the table and then ran his calloused fingers through the hair of his charges.

After a few seconds of careful peering and pinching, he satisfied himself that they were well.

The boys were so hungry, they began to eat at once, firing questions at Peter between mouthfuls. What was happening outside, they wanted to know, and was there any chance they would be released?

Unfortunately, Peter's answers were disappointing. He knew little of life out-

115

side the Tower, and he did not hold out any hope that they would be set free soon.

The Constable seemed to be having more visitors of late, he said, but whether that had anything to do with his royal charges or not, he was not sure.

Three men in particular had been visiting Sir Robert — Sir James Tyrell, a wealthy landowner and friend of the new king, his servant John Dighton, and a rough-looking fellow named Miles Forest.

"Twice they have toured the Tower with the Constable," Peter said. "Both times, they have been particularly interested in a stone staircase being rebuilt at the White Tower. Why, I do not know."

He had nothing else to report.

Then several days later on another rare visit, Peter did have some news that was of interest to the boys.

"The king has left London," the servant said. "They say he has gone to Warwick Castle. No one knows how long he will be there."

The information intrigued Edward. After Peter had gone, he pondered over it.

That castle is comfortable, he thought to himself, and the country would be a change from London, but I'm surprised my uncle would go there now. His power is here, and he needs to establish it firmly. I suppose it may be that he wants to show himself to the people — yet the timing is odd and he is not a foolish man. He must be up to something.

Gradually Edward became more and more unsettled. His uncle, he now had no doubt, was capable of anything.

All that day, Edward kept his thoughts to himself. But when the brothers lay in bed that night and long shadows played silently over the stone walls, his fears finally got the better of him and he began to shiver violently. Those shadows looked too much like ghostly hangmen to him.

Beside him, Richard stirred.

"What is wrong, brother?" he said.

Edward, feeling the presence of death in the still of the night, spoke like the frightened twelve-year-old he really was.

"I'm terribly afraid, Richard," he said.

"Afraid of what?"

"Of what Richard may do."

There, it was out. Now he could tell his brother everything.

"What do you mean?" prompted Richard.

"I mean we should be on our guard, Richard. Even though there is little we can really do to protect ourselves, we will have to try. Before he died, Dr. Alcock confided in me his worst fears. I was shocked by what he said and did not want to believe him, but I'm afraid he may have been right."

"What fears?" Richard's voice was taut and high.

"He was convinced the Protector was going to steal the crown." Edward's voice

118

was little more than a whisper. "But, more than that, he feared for my life. Oh, little brother, I'm so sorry to say this, but now that we are both here together, Richard may kill us — or have us killed."

Richard did not respond at first, sitting still and silent beside his brother on the oversize bed. Then suddenly tears streamed down his face.

"I want my mother!" he wailed. "She won't let him hurt us. I want my mother!"

"But she might not even know," Edward said softly. "If they kill us here, we could be dead for weeks, even years, before she would know. They could tell her we were safely locked up in the Tower. We both know she cannot come here. If she did, she would be locked up with us."

"What shall we do then, brother?" Richard asked tremulously. "When will they come?"

"I do not know what we will do when they come," Edward replied, "but I think they will come soon. England does not need me."

"But what can we do?" Richard repeated, his voice breaking.

"We can pray," said Edward. "And we can try to protect each other. If they only send one person, we may be able to do something."

He drew the covers closer round himself.

"I will be their first target," he continued, his voice low. "I think we can be sure of that."

"We need weapons of some sort," Richard put in suddenly. "Then we can surprise anyone who comes in here."

As he spoke, his glance fell on a three-legged stool by a window.

"Let's take that stool apart," he said. "The legs will make good clubs."

Within seconds, the two boys were armed with makeshift clubs. They were not big, but they were sturdy and easy to handle.

"Look, brother," Richard cried. "Look!"

He stood in the moonlight coming in through the window and swung his club wildly, shouting at the top of his voice.

"Come on, you traitors," he roared. "Come on! Come and get me if you dare! We'll pound your brains to porridge. We'll smash your faces into a bloody pulp. You'll *never* get me, or my brother. He is the real king. Just try to hurt us. Harm us and you will die!"

Richard raced around the room brandishing his club and screaming dire threats at anyone foolish enough to come near him.

Edward laughed in spite of himself. He cheered his brother on, then lunged towards him, pretending to attack. A minute later, they were wrestling on the floor, lost for a moment to the deadly reality of their game.

Suddenly, there was a sound on the stairs.

Edward leaped to his feet, his hand

tight on his club, crying, "Oh, dear God, protect us!"

"It is your servant," came a gravelly voice through the door.

"It's Peter," said Richard, and he ran to the door.

The boys had not seen anyone in two days.

"Come in, Peter, come in and tell us . . ."

Richard's words died on his lips.

A huge stranger stood before them, an old dented tray with a loaf of bread and a jug of water on it in one hand, a sputtering candle in the other. He grunted, banged the tray down on the table and looked around. Edward darted across the room and stood in front of him.

"Just who are you?" asked the boy. "Where is Peter?"

The stranger stopped, straightened to his full height and glared down at Edward, light from the candle reflecting in his eyes. They were deeply set in a fleshy face above a beard stained with tobacco juice. Hot, foul-smelling breath wafted over Edward and almost sickened him. He instinctively turned away.

"Where is Peter?" the boy repeated. "And who are you?"

The giant belched in reply.

Richard cowered against a far wall, his face white and his hands shaking.

"Who are you?" Edward tried again, now as disgusted as he was afraid. "Why are you here? Where is Peter? Bring Peter here."

The huge man looked down at the boy and sneered. Then he spat on the floor and laughed loudly, his enormous belly jiggling. Again he belched, this time directly into Edward's face.

The boy did not back down.

"Where is Peter?" he demanded.

The man's laughter came to a sudden stop. He glared at Edward, then without warning brought a huge, hairy hand up from his side and slapped him hard on the side of the face. Edward's head snapped to one side and he collapsed in a heap on the floor.

Richard wailed in terror.

"Peter is in the dungeons where he belongs," snarled the giant. "*I* will see to you now. And remember, you are only a stripling prince — and not one His Majesty particularly cares for."

With that, he stalked from the room and locked the door behind him.

For a few seconds, neither boy moved. Finally Edward managed to sit up, his head throbbing with pain, his bottom lip bleeding. He said nothing, so shocked was he by the blow he had received.

Richard spoke first, his voice shaking.

"Brother, are you all right?" he whispered, still pressed into the corner.

Edward nodded his head slowly, his hand pressed against his swollen face.

"Yes, but my head hurts terribly."

Tears welled in his eyes and he tasted blood in his mouth.

The younger prince got up at last and went to his brother's side.

"Let me see," he said softly.

The little princes huddled together in the darkness, each thinking of Peter, locked away because he had been a loyal and kind servant to them. They had lost their only friend.

At last the weak rays of the morning sun lit up their room and the boys rose as one. They did not touch the food. They found it hard to do anything at all, other than to sit listlessly on the side of the bed in fearful silence.

Finally Richard asked, his voice trembling, "Edward, will we die tonight?"

Edward tried to be comforting, determined to overcome his own fear so that he might ease his brother's terror.

"No, of course not. They have probably decided to leave us here. No doubt they took Peter because they thought he would let us go. It is possible they learned of the plans he made with Dr. Alcock for my escape."

All day, the older boy kept talking — about escape, about outwitting the guards, about scaling the wall. The planning and dreaming gave him courage and stilled his brother's trembling a little.

"We have our clubs," he said. "It is still possible they may try to kill us, but they won't succeed, Richard. Just you watch. We'll be ready for them. We must stay alert so that no one can sneak up on us unawares. We had better stay awake tonight."

And stay awake they did, till long after the candle had sputtered and died. But as the hours passed, the silence and darkness of the night blanketed their fears and made danger seem less real. Far away in the streets of the city a dog barked, but deep inside the brick and stone Tower of London, all was still.

The little princes yawned and yawned again. Finally, late in the night,

126

they drifted into a sound asleep, convinced after their long vigil that they were still safe, at least for one more night.

*   *   *

Their sleep would not have been so sound, however, if they had they known what had taken place at Warwick Castle a few days previously when King Richard had arrived there.

Their uncle had held a secret meeting with a few of his closest allies. Present were Robert Brackenbury, Constable of the Tower, and the men Peter had seen so often of late — Sir James Tyrell, John Dighton and Miles Forest.

The meeting lasted half a day. When it ended, Brackenbury and his companions took leave of their sovereign and set out for London.

As they rode back to the city, the four men reviewed their plans for the murder they had agreed to carry out. It would be quick. The disposal of the bodies was all arranged. Excavation for construction of the new staircase at the White Tower was complete. The gaping hole would be filled with rock as a base for the new steps. No one need ever know there was more than rock under those stairs . . .

"But what of the servant?" Dighton had asked as they stood by a stream to water the horses. "He knows those boys and he might warn them."

"Or put up a fight," Forest added.

"He will do no such thing," said Tyrell. "Robert has already taken care of him."

Dighton and Forest looked at Brackenbury.

"Peter was really too old for his job," explained the Constable evenly. "I replaced him with a fellow we can trust. Peter won't be warning anyone."

The conspirators laughed, pleased that the Constable was one of them. He had left nothing to chance. In return for his cooperation, the Constable would return to his own quarters without ever entering the princes' chamber. That way he hoped his name would never be linked to the terrible deed.

"Once the door is open," the Constable went on, "you, Tyrell, will guard it. Dighton and Forest, you will carry out the act and then take the bodies away. Afterwards, the servant will put the room in order."

The men agreed readily. Only Forest seemed at all troubled.

"Let us ensure that their death is swift," he muttered. "They are only boys and I do not wish to see them suffer."

*   *   *

In the darkness of the Tower, the boys slept on. Suddenly, Edward awakened, hardly daring to breathe. He had felt, rather than heard, a step on the stair. Beside him, Richard snored softly, oblivious.

The young prince peered into the gloom, straining his ears for a sound. With one hand, he slowly reached under his pillow for his club. As he did so, he shook his brother, alerting him to danger.

Richard awoke with a start and went to sit up. Edward grabbed his arm. The younger boy understood at once and lay back, wide-eyed with terror.

A few seconds later, the door to their room began to open slowly.

Chapter 10

The little princes clung to each other and watched in silent horror as a hulking shape entered the room and slipped to one side. Then a second followed the first, and a third stayed motionless in the doorway.

The two boys lay back in terror, too afraid to do more. Edward grasped his little brother's hand in a wordless entreaty that they would soon be together in heaven.

Outside, a mournful wind swept over the battlements and rattled the windows. Across the Thames a dagger of lightning split the sky. Moments later the rumble of thunder rolled over the Tower walls.

The lightning came again, nearer, brilliant as an exploding star. Briefly it lit up the room where the two little boys lay hand in hand, awaiting death. By its light they saw for one terrifying second the faces of their murderers.

When darkness returned, the killers moved swiftly to the royal bedside.

For an instant, nothing happened.

Edward's hand tightened on his club. Richard forgot he had one. Instead, in that fraction of time when his attackers loomed motionless and huge, he lifted up the blankets and ducked under them.

In one swift motion, Dighton grabbed hold of Edward's pillow and forced it down over the boy's face. Edward struggled and kicked frantically, waving his little club wildly and pathetically in the air. Dighton held on, pushing down firmly, inexorably, on the pillow while thunder crashed outside.

Richard, grappling with Forest, screamed in terror. Then the killer pressed a pillow against the younger boy's face too, smothering his cries for help.

"Be still!" he murmured. "By

heaven's grace, be still and let there be an end to it."

It was several long minutes before the struggling finally subsided and Forest and Dighton were able to stagger to their feet.

Only then did Tyrell light a torch.

By its blood-red glow, the murderers gazed in silence at the small, contorted bodies on the ravaged bed.

It was Tyrell who finally spoke.

"Pick them up," he said quietly. "The deed is done."

Afterword

It was thus that Richard III secured for himself the throne of England. There are those who say he was the most terrifying man ever to wear the English crown. Others maintain history has done him an injustice. Certainly, his reign was both controversial and brief. Intrigue and slaughter surrounded him. He himself was killed in the Battle of Bosworth at the age of 32 while defending his crown against the armies of Henry Tudor. He had reigned for only two years.

One hundred and ninety-one years after the deaths of the princes, workmen were making repairs to sections of the Tower. In particular, a staircase at the south side of the White Tower was torn down so that it could be replaced by a newer structure.

During the excavation, small human

bones were found in a chest below the base of the old stone stairs. At first, the discovery was dismissed as unimportant and the remains were tossed aside.

Later, however, people who knew the story of the princes brought the grisly find to the attention of the reigning monarch, King Charles II. He ordered the bones examined by the royal surgeon, who came to the conclusion that they were the skeletons of Edward and Richard. King Charles commissioned the renowned architect Sir Christopher Wren to design a vessel to hold them.

In due course Wren fashioned a beautiful urn of white marble and the bones were placed inside. The urn was taken to Westminster Abbey, where it remains to this day.